THAW

RICK JASPER

brazio

NIGHT FALL

THAW

RICK JASPER

MINNEAPOLIS

GRAND RAPIDS PUBLIC LIBRARY

Darby Creek
A division of Lerner Publishing Group, Inc.
241 First Avenue North
Minneapolis, MN 55401 U.S.A.

Website address: www.lernerbooks.com

Cover design: Becky Daum
Cover photograph: iStockphoto; Roger McClean/
iStockphoto

Jasper, Rick, 1948–
Thaw / by Rick Jasper.
p.   cm. — (Night fall)
ISBN 978-0-7613-6145-9 (lib. bdg. : alk. paper)
[1. Horror stories.] I. Title.
PZ7.J32Th 2010
[Fic]—dc22   2010003323

Manufactured in the United States of America
1—BP—7/15/10

For N.,
who believed I could
actually do this

Deep into that darkness peering, long I stood there wondering, fearing,
Doubting, dreaming dreams no mortal ever dared to dream before

—*Edgar Allan Poe,* The Raven

I didn't know it then, but it all began with a wild thunderstorm in July. Trees blew down and two people were killed. Lightning struck a power station and all of Bridgewater lost electricity for a couple of days. Days with highs in the nineties.

When the power came back, all the news on TV was about the damage, people suffering without air conditioning, food spoiling, people driving fifty miles around closed roads to find someplace where the gas pumps and their cell phones worked. The biggest story, though, the one that made national news, involved the

Institute for Cryonic Experimentation, or ICE. It was on all the networks. In fact, you can still find some of the reports online. I did.

Here's an early one:

"WBNE has just learned about a gruesome sidelight to the storm and power outage in the town of Bridgewater. Our Megan Rodriguez is on the scene. Megan, what's going on there?"

"Well, Buck, you can see the one-story brick building behind me. It looks quite ordinary, but federal agents have descended on this building in the last twenty-four hours, and residents of Bridgewater have learned about a bizarre research project that's been going on here for years. I have FBI Agent Joe . . . Sir, how do you pronounce your last name?"

"Felice. Rhymes with police."

". . . Agent Joe Felice. Agent Felice, can you tell us what this building was used for?"

"It's a cryonic facility, ma'am. The government has been studying the effects of super-low temperatures on human tissue."

"And we've learned that the human tissue was provided by deceased federal prisoners, isn't that right?"

"Yes, ma'am. Several inmates who died while incarcerated and who had signed donation consent forms were subjects of the research."

"How many?"

"Twenty-seven, ma'am."

"For how long?"

"Going on fifteen years now."

"Agent Felice, we've all heard stories about the wealthy having their bodies frozen in the hope of being restored at a future time. But why would the federal government be involved in this?"

"I'm afraid I can't release that information, ma'am."

"There has been speculation that this involved NASA research into deep-space travel."

"I'd respectfully offer no comment on that."

"Let me ask a different question, then. Is it true that one of the deceased inmates used in this research was the infamous cult leader Ted 'Scatter' Olson?"

"Yes, ma'am, he was one of the first."

"Wasn't it Scatter Olson who was locked up for life years ago? Didn't he influence his followers to commit armed robbery and ritual murder?"

"That's correct, ma'am."

"Agent Felice, was the facility affected by the power outage?"

"Yes, ma'am. The backup generator—you know, like you have in a hospital in case power fails?—that failed as well."

"So the subjects of this research, uh, thawed out?"

"Presumably, ma'am."

"Can you describe the scene? I'd imagine decaying corpses would create quite a stink."

"No smell, ma'am."

"But in this heat, wouldn't the bodies be decomposing rapidly?"

"No bodies, ma'am."

"I beg your pardon?"

"That's what we're investigating, ma'am. The bodies are gone."

Pretty interesting, I guess. I paid attention at the time. But I forgot about it quickly, because a day later my best friend disappeared.

My name is Danielle Kraft. My friends call me Dani. And my best friend, the one who disappeared, is Jake Sawyer. Jake and I have always joked that we were twins. We were born on the same day a little more than sixteen years ago. I was born in Bridgewater and Jake in Israel. His dad was there for two years studying ancient languages. Jake didn't remember the place; he was a baby when his parents moved to Bridgewater and his dad started teaching at Noble College.

We started hanging out in sixth grade,

when I was still taller than he was. Jake was a pudgy kid then, but cute, with wild black curls and glittery blue eyes you thought could almost glow in the dark. It was in sixth grade that we figured out we had the same birthday and that we were both only children. And we had something else in common, although to this day we haven't named it. It's like a special awareness of each other. We can always tell without talking how the other person is feeling, and when we do talk we have to make an effort not to finish each other's sentences.

By the time we got to high school we might as well have been twins. We texted constantly and worked on school projects together whenever we could. We were both on our school's swim team. We both had other friends but . . . I don't know. Maybe, for each other, we were the siblings we didn't have at home.

Of course we both got teased as we got older, as Jake got skinnier and gained six inches on me. Like my friend Alexa, for example, who's always raging, "Dani, you are so in denial! You guys are in love!" I swear it's not like that, though. In some ways it's almost like we're still sixth-graders. We just like hanging out. We're easy together. In the mornings at school we'd always hug the first time we saw each other, as if we were glad to see the other had made it through the night.

In the summers I didn't see Jake as often. We both had jobs, mine at the country club and his at the supermarket. But we phoned and texted. Either one of us could always tell you what the other's day had been like. Until the storm. When the power came back I texted, I called—no answer. He wasn't online.

At first I was impatient, then worried. On the third day of nothing, I biked over to Jake's house across town. The family car was in the driveway, but the house looked as if no one lived there. No one answered the door, even though I practically banged it down. I looked in the windows. Nothing. I called the supermarket, and they said Jake hadn't been in since before the storm. But they hadn't been open. They were still cleaning up the mess.

At some point then I just started to lose it. How could he just disappear like that? I couldn't sleep at night. I started crying all the time. Every time my phone rang, I'd jump. Then I'd be annoyed with whoever was calling because it wasn't Jake.

By the second week, in between my tears, I was angry. What kind of a friend would do this to me? The anger finally gave way to just a sick, sad feeling whenever I thought about him and the prospect of going through the rest of my life without any answers.

Alexa was totally wrong. Jake and I were just friends. But my heart was breaking anyway.

Then, on a Wednesday more than three weeks after Jake vanished, I had a visitor.

That Wednesday Mom and Dad had left for their annual week in Maine with a couple they'd known since college. So I was home alone that night when I heard the doorbell. Through the locked screen door I faced a man on our porch. You know when your parents tell you not to talk to strangers? This guy looked like the strangers they have in mind. Tall, thin, dirty, with a stringy black beard and eyes that wouldn't stay still. Stained, baggy jeans and a gray hoodie that matched his skin. When he spoke, I saw that he was missing about half his teeth.

"You would be Danielle Kraft?" he asked.

"Why do you want to know?"

The missing teeth caused him to whistle on the "s" sounds when he said, "I'm a friend of the Sawyers."

Just hearing the name made my eyes start to get watery. I was such a wimp. Would the tears ever go away? "The Sawyers are gone," I said and started to close the door.

"Almost."

"What did you say? What do you mean?!"

"Jake said you were his best friend."

"You talked to Jake?! When?"

"You are Danielle, then?"

I gave in. Somehow, this guy didn't frighten me. He just kind of grossed me out. "Okay," I said. "Let's talk out here." I unhooked the screen door, turned on the porch light, and stepped outside. The light made the man squint, and it gave me a better look at him.

His skin, which had looked gray in the shadows, was gray only in splotches. In places it was a raw red, and in others, like his nose, the gray was almost black. It reminded me of something familiar; I just couldn't quite pin it down. And he was missing more than teeth. Several fingers and the ends of fingers were gone from both hands, and he had lost an ear.

"What's your name?" I asked. "What do you know about Jake?"

He kept looking over his shoulder, as if he were afraid of being watched.

"Call me Vincent," he whistled. "I spoke to Jake a week ago. I tried to help him. Now . . ." He looked sadly at the floor. "I'm afraid I may have done the opposite."

"If you've hurt him . . ."

"Not me. Does the name 'Scatter' mean anything to you?"

"Uh, dead guy in the news? His body was frozen at the cryo place. Now it's missing? What does he have to do with anything?"

"You are too young to remember when Scatter was . . . here. He had a large following."

"It sounded like he was a creep."

"To those of us . . . to his followers, he seemed to be . . . . Right, wrong—Scatter seemed to be beyond all that."

"He went to prison."

"Yes, one of his followers betrayed him. Gave a certain government official information about his activities."

"Like killing people?"

"'This world cannot understand me.' Scatter said that many times. And he said he would die in chains because of that, but return to confront his enemies."

"This has nothing to do with Jake," I said.

"I'm afraid it does. The person who betrayed Scatter was Philip Sawyer, Jake's father."

I started to feel sick. "And now . . . ?"

"Scatter has returned, as he promised, and when the frozen were returned to life, he acquired new followers."

"Has he hurt Jake or his parents? Has he killed them?"

"They live, but I can't be sure how much longer. They are in Scatter's world now."

"Scatter's world? Seriously. What are you even *talking* about?"

"Young lady, there are many worlds. And there are those, like Scatter, who know how to move among them."

This was all too much. I was an idiot. I was so worried about Jake that I had almost bought into this nut case, Vincent.

"Look," I said, "this is all bull. You're feeding me something out of a cheap horror movie. How do I know if any of this is true?"

Silently, Vincent reached under his shirt, pulled out a brown envelope, and offered it to me. As I took the package that would change my life forever, I realized what Vincent's skin looked like. Freezer burn.

Inside the envelope was a DVD. I put it in
my laptop and, for the first time in almost a
month, I was looking at my best friend. He was
in his room at home.

"Dani," he said, "if you're seeing this, you're
probably pretty pissed at me." He had that
right. "But the thing I'm about to do is really
messed up," he continued. "And it's a family
thing. I can't pull you into it. Anyway, I think I
can do it on my own. You'll only be seeing this
in case I couldn't.

"If you're watching this, then you've met

Vincent. Maybe he explained a little bit to you already. The morning after the storm, when everyone woke up without power, I woke up without my parents. The car was here. Nothing seemed out of place. But Mom and Dad were gone. No note. I called Dad before I realized the phones weren't working. Then I thought maybe they'd gone for a walk. The neighborhood was full of people checking out the damage. But I asked around everywhere, and no one had seen any trace of Mom or Dad.

"You know, Dani, I'm not that close with them, but it's so weird when they're gone for no reason. You start thinking, 'What if they never come back?' I thought about calling the police."

Why didn't you think about calling me? I thought, and immediately felt selfish.

"Then there was someone at the door, and I thought maybe it was them. But it was Vincent, with the story about Scatter, and Mom and Dad's days in the cult. Vincent thinks I can find them in this other world, and he says he'll help me. I'm going to try.

"It's funny, even before the storm, for the last week they'd been acting kind of strange."

What was funny about that was that Jake's parents acting strange was like the pope acting Catholic. How those two managed to have a kid as normal as Jake was an ongoing mystery to me. They were in another world a long time before their disappearance.

I'd heard my dad call them hippies. Dr. Sawyer was dark like Jake, but short and powerful. His eyes were black, and even when he smiled they drilled into you like the eyes of some actor in a silent film. He couldn't make normal conversation; he blinked and nodded like the real world in front of him was some kind of odd entertainment. Jake's mom—that's where he got his blue eyes and maybe his tall, thin build—was blond and hyper. She was always busy, running around, like something was chasing her.

Jake went on. "I'm hoping you'll never see this, Dani, and we'll be back in touch in a day or two.

But I asked Vincent to give you this disc if he didn't hear from me in three weeks."

And then came the part that, of course, made me melt into tears: "Hey, twin sister, I love you. Whatever happens, I hope you know that."

"Whatever happens?!" I yelled at the screen. "Dammit, Jake, why didn't you call me?!"

After a while, I just tried to think. I replayed the recording. Three times. Then once more. And something was wrong. What the heck was the matter? Was it his voice? His expression? I knew Jake almost as well as I know myself. And something was off. I couldn't pin it down. The guy on the DVD was definitely Jake. But somehow, it wasn't.

I had to start putting some of this together.
So I googled Scatter. Born Theodore Harlan
Olson in 1950 in Boise, Idaho. Ordinary family:
Dad worked at the post office. Mom taught
kindergarten. One sibling, a younger brother.

In 1970 Ted was a college student. He was
drafted into the army, but serious asthma got
him a deferment. Three years later he was in
Egypt, a graduate student in archaeology. That
was the first time he got into trouble. In 1974
Egypt deported him back to the U.S., and he
was kicked out of his grad program for trying to
steal ancient artifacts.

No one heard from him for the rest of the seventies. But he surfaced in upstate New York in 1981. By then he was the leader of two or three dozen "disciples"—people in their teens and twenties, plus a few children. That's when he took the name Scatter. The cult lived on an abandoned farm. The members supported themselves by begging in nearby towns, doing odd jobs and—it wasn't known then—robbery.

The group worshipped Scatter. First thing every morning he would preach to them. Then he'd send them out to do their work. There would be another service in the evening after dinner. On Sundays he'd preach all day. His message was pretty standard cult stuff: He had been anointed by God to save a chosen few from the wicked world. He was destined to be persecuted and killed, but he would return in triumph and reward his followers. He demanded absolute loyalty from all. That included the women in the cult, who were expected to sleep with him if so ordered.

Over the years, it was rumored that the group had stashed a lot of money. Now and then the leader would even refer to "Scatter's treasure," claiming he would divide it among his followers on his after-death return.

But things went south in 1993, when an anonymous tip led police to a gravesite near the cult campground. There they found the bodies of the family—parents and three children—who had supposedly abandoned the farm years before.

All five had been mummified. Their organs were removed and put in jars, and their bodies were soaked in salt water and wrapped in cloth saturated in plaster. They were arranged like the spokes of an uneven wheel. Their feet touched at the center; the organ jars stood by the head of each.

Ah, the heads. The medical examiner learned that, in fact, the bodies had been decapitated. Each mummy contained a body and a head that didn't match. The dad's body was embalmed with the mom's head and so on. And the organ jar next to each mummy belonged to yet a third family member.

It wasn't long before evidence of cult involvement in various crimes over the previous dozen years began to turn up. Soon the whole group was arrested. A few confessed to murder or robbery. All said, proudly, that they had been ordered to do these things by Scatter. To them, that meant they'd been directed by God.

In 1994, Scatter was given life in prison for his role in the crimes, even though there was no proof he'd committed any of them with his own hands. A year later he died in prison and, I know now, was frozen in Bridgewater.

The authorities, as well as some amateur treasure hunters, searched the cult compound for years, but no money was ever found.

I knew that Vincent would be back before long. He had acted as if he thought I could help Jake and his family. And for whatever reason, he seemed to want me to try. If not for the

DVD, I would have called the police. Even with the DVD, that's what a sensible person would have done. But the problem was that, since Jake was gone, I wasn't sensible. I wanted to believe Vincent, even though he gave me the creeps and his story was ridiculous. Resurrected corpses kidnapping human beings and transporting them to "another world"? Yeah, that sounds totally legit.

Suppose for a minute I swallowed Vincent's story. Suppose Vincent, who had already sent Jake into a place where he was lost, wanted me to follow him. In my mind, I tried to list the pros and cons.

Con:

1. If I went into this, I could be in serious danger. This come-back-to-life dead guy was a criminal.

2. I could get stuck in never-never land like Jake and never come back.

3. What about Mom and Dad? Did I just disappear and leave a note like, "I'm going to

Scatter's world to rescue Jake and his parents. It might be a few weeks. Luv ya!"?

4. Who was Vincent, anyway? Maybe he was some weirdo who had killed Jake and his family and now was toying with me.

Pro:

1. If Jake and his parents were with Scatter now, they were in danger. Jake might need me.

Four cons, one pro. Okay. I was going.

The next day was Thursday. I was the lifeguard on duty at the Bridgewater Country Club pool. That day the duty was light, though. A cold front had moved through overnight. The day was windy and around sixty degrees, despite the sunlight. While the pool was officially open, there was no one in the water. I was perched in the lifeguard chair, wearing a track suit over my swimsuit to stay warm. I was writing a paper on my laptop. School would start in a few weeks, and my journal on the summer reading list would be due on day one.

My attention was split. Writing my paper? Check. No one on the verge of jumping into the pool and drowning? Check. And every few minutes I'd look up to see if Vincent was around. Now that I'd decided to look for Jake, I was impatient to get started.

"Dani!"

I looked up, hopeful, but it was only Trey Little. Blond, conceited, annoying Trey Little. Trey—Charles Winston Little, III—was a member of what people in Bridgewater called "the Nobility." That meant his family was related to the oldest, richest clan in the town, the Nobles.

Trey wasn't a bad guy, really. I just didn't share his high opinion of himself. He considered himself a "chick magnet." And it was true. He was great looking, played on the football team. A lot of girls bought into his act. Trouble was, Trey only wanted what he couldn't have, and that included me.

"Hey, beautiful! Isn't it cold up there?"

"Whatever, Trey. I'm working on a paper."

"Lunch break in ten minutes. Wanna grab a burger? I've got the Audi."

"I'm expecting someone." I tried to look busy.

"Hey, sometimes the best company is the unexpected kind. C'mon!"

"Look, Trey, I'm . . ."

"Danielle! It's Vincent." The voice hissed from the shrubs just outside the pool gate.

Trey's eyes got wide. "You seeing homeless guys now?"

I jumped down from the chair. "I told you, Trey, I'm expecting someone. See you around."

But Trey had gone over to the gate. "This is members only," he said to Vincent. "Are you going to leave, or do I need to call security?"

Vincent said something to him that I couldn't hear. But when Trey turned around, his face was white. He looked at me for a moment, then he scurried off.

I told Vincent to wait a minute, ran down to the locker room, and put my stuff away. When I got back I said, "Trey probably will call security. I'm going on break. Let's go across the road."

We walked across the club driveway and down to Folly Park, several acres of lawn and trees with paved pathways winding through. With the cold weather, the place was almost deserted. Just a couple of bundled-up moms with jogging strollers roamed around.

"Vincent, what did you say to Trey back there?"

"I told him something about himself that he thought no one knew."

I wasn't curious. It was Trey.

We found a bench near some trees and sat down. "Okay," I said. "Do you think I can help Jake?"

Vincent shook his head. "I can only help you to enter Scatter's world. Finding your friend, bringing him back—you'll have to figure that out on your own. I told Jake the same thing when he went after his parents."

"Suppose I find him. How will I get back here?"

"It should be just like going in. That's what I explained to Jake. But something must have gone wrong, because the paw came back to me."

"The paw?"

Vincent reached into the pocket of his hoodie and pulled out something black and dried-up looking. It was bigger than a rabbit's foot and not at all fuzzy, but it was part of a leg with a paw at the end. A cat's paw.

"This is the key to Scatter's world," Vincent said as he handed the paw to me. No sooner had I taken it than it started to move. It got warm in my hand, and the toes stretched apart and the claws came out, just like the paw of a live cat.

I screamed, and the paw fell softly to the ground. "Why is it doing that?!"

"The paw is a relic," Vincent said. "It's thousands of years old. It moves in your hand because it senses your heart is light. It did the same thing for Jake."

A light heart? Not lately. What was he talking about?

Vincent calmly picked up the paw and put it

back in my hand. The paw continued to squirm, but I managed not to drop it.

"Look around you," Vincent said. "Do you see anything unusual?"

The park looked the same as always, lush and green. But then, in the trees right behind us . . . . I rubbed my eyes and looked again. Part of the greenery had become liquid, shimmery, as if I were seeing it through tears.

"That's an entryway," Vincent said. "Give me the paw." I handed it back to him, and immediately it became stiff and dry, like an old stick. "Look at the entryway again," Vincent said.

It was gone. I shot a questioning glance at Vincent.

"There's one problem with the paw," he said. "It can lead you to Scatter, but it can also lead Scatter to you. When you hold it, he will sense your presence. If you lose it, it will return to me."

"And Jake lost it," I said.

"I fear so." He handed the paw back to me.

"Why are you helping me? Why did you try to help Jake?"

Vincent paused for a moment. "I believe in innocence," he said. "Scatter uses innocence. I want to stop that."

"Why don't you go after him?"

"There are reasons. My heart is heavy, I'm afraid." He seemed distracted by his thoughts for a moment. Then he spoke again. "Danielle, this will be a journey full of dangers. Scatter will test you. I guarantee there will be times you want to turn back. Those are the times to remember your love for your friend. Scatter can manipulate appearances. But he can't manipulate your heart."

Squeezing the paw, I walked toward the gateway among the trees. I looked back one last time as I went into the shimmering place. Vincent was waving his arms. He seemed to be shouting "No!" but I couldn't hear him. At the same time, a hand gripped my arm, and darkness surrounded me.

was standing at the edge of a huge lake in the middle of a dead forest. I could have been in the hilly woods that surrounded Bridgewater, except that the trees were gray and bare and broken. The brush was scarce, and fine dust covered the ground. It was nighttime. The air was mild, and moonlight made the water look like silver. The only sound was the lake lapping at the shore.

And someone breathing. Someone right next to me. Trey Little.

"What the hell, Trey!" I yelled at him. "What did you think you were doing?!"

"What did *you* think *you* were doing?" he answered. It turned out that Trey had sneaked across the road and into the trees to spy on my meeting with Vincent. When he saw me starting to disappear, he dived in.

We stared each other down for a moment, and finally I just started to laugh. The paw was still in my hand.

"Trey, let's talk." There was a fallen tree trunk nearby that worked as a bench. "I really don't know how to explain all this, Trey, but it doesn't involve you. Look. Let's just go back to the park. I'll drop you off."

"Dani, don't. I don't know what's going on, but I can help."

"How?" No answer. "Okay, fine. I'm looking for Jake Sawyer. He's my best friend, and he hasn't been heard from for weeks. That's all I'm here for. If you're going to tag along, you need to understand that. And we're going to be in serious danger. We're not on some kind of adventure date here, okay?"

He nodded eagerly. So I sighed and gave

him the short version of what had happened since the storm. When I finished, he shook his head. Trey, of all people, actually seemed a little sad.

"Wow," he said. "Sawyer's lucky to have a friend like you."

"So you see, Trey," I tried once more, "you really don't need to get involved in this." I reached into my pocket and held the paw. Immediately the air just a few yards away turned watery. "Here, just walk right this way and you'll be back at the country club before you can blink."

He looked at me solemnly. "Let me stay, Dani. Seriously. I'm cool with you and Jake. Maybe I can help."

I wasn't convinced. But at that point the wind began to kick up and the lake started churning. Big waves broke among the pieces of driftwood on the shore. And in the distance we could see some kind of craft approaching. It was a raft with a triangular sail. A white, glowing figure stood by a rudder, steering it toward us. Before long the raft was on the beach, and a figure in a white, hooded robe beckoned us to come closer.

All I could see of its face were dark holes where eyes and nose and a mouth would be. Whether the face itself was bone or dead flesh I couldn't be sure. The beckoning hand was wrapped, each finger individually, in dirty cloth. When Trey and I were close, the figure stretched out its hand toward me and flexed its fingers repeatedly. The way the cat's paw did when I held it. I reached in and showed the paw. The figure nodded and motioned for us to board the raft.

Soon we were in the middle of the lake, tossing on the waves. Trey put an arm around my shoulder to keep us steady. I wondered if Scatter already knew we were here.

The lake featured a large expanse of open water, with countless bays and tiny islands in all directions. From the air, I thought, it would have looked like an amoeba. After an hour or so, our boatman steered into a narrow channel that opened onto a bay. It was surrounded, like the rest of the lake, with the white, splintered bones of trees. In the distance I could see two bright lights. They reminded me of the spotlights you see fixed on poles in farmyards.

Silhouetted in the moonlight nearer the shore was an old diving platform. One edge sank lower than the other, and a couple of dirty buoys bumped against it. It was as if they had broken loose and drifted there in the current.

"It looks like some kind of summer camp," Trey said as the boatman brought the raft around and tied it to a rickety dock.

"A long time ago," I said. "But no one's taken care of it in a while."

The hooded figure stayed on the raft but gestured for us to get off. As soon as Trey and I were on the dock, the boatman shoved off, sailing back the way we had come.

"What now?" Trey asked.

I took out the paw, and it stretched straight ahead, in the direction of the lights. I could see now that they were on top of a ridge several hundred yards away. "That way," I said, and Trey followed.

It was just as we set foot on the shore that we noticed the smell.

It was like we'd smacked into a wall of decaying flesh. We both started to gag and jumped back on the dock.

"Oh, man!" Trey gasped. "What is that?"

As if in answer, several dozen small figures emerged from the darkness and began running toward us. They were children, dripping wet and covered in green slime. They didn't make a sound, but their mouths opened and closed, like the mouths of fish out of water. Their eyes seemed to be pleading with us. As they got closer, I saw that their bodies and faces were bloated and beginning to rot. In some places the skin was coming off their bones.

When they got to the dock, they stopped. For what seemed like an eternity, they stared at us. At first they seemed hopeful, like pets expecting to be fed, then desperate.

"What do you want?!" I cried.

But they only gazed at us through dead eyes until, finally, their shoulders slumped. They turned away and retreated back into the shadows.

"This place is messed up." Trey looked shaken. "It was like they were saying, 'Help us!'" he said.

"But they looked . . ." I didn't know quite how to say it. ". . . beyond help."

Trey and I stepped off the dock again and headed for the lights. With only moonlight to guide us, we picked our way among rocks and dead branches.

About halfway to our goal, we saw an old sign nailed to a tree. It read: "John 3:16." Fifty yards farther was another sign, yellow and diamond shaped. In black letters it said, "Jesus at Work."

By then we could see several buildings surrounded by a wire fence. The camp looked a little like a minimum-security prison. Then there was another sign, very worn and hard to read in the shadows: "Rock of Ages Bible Camp." Trey and I let out the same swear word at once. Everyone in Bridgewater knew the story of Rock of Ages, even though the tragedy was decades old.

It was sometime in the seventies. Rock of Ages was a big operation. Hundreds of kids attended every summer. They came to fish, swim, enjoy "fellowship," and, of course, sing hymns and study the Bible. A lot of kids my age had parents who'd summered there as campers or counselors.

One August afternoon, almost the entire camp set out on a couple of pontoons for a picnic on the far side of the lake. The weather was hot and still, and the sky was an odd color. On the TV and radio, there were warnings about the chance of severe storms, but TV and radio were banned in the camp.

About the time the campers hit open water on the big lake, hail and lightning and high winds came ripping through the woods. That was followed by a tornado that knocked down most of the trees in a path a mile wide. The boats never had a chance. They capsized, and forty-three people, mostly children, drowned.

The aftermath was bad: failed rescue attempts, funerals for bodies never recovered, government safety investigations, and lawsuits. The harsh spotlight fell on the camp director. He had not been at the picnic. It turned out that he had embezzled thousands from the camp, then disappeared on the day of the tragedy. He'd been heard to say early that morning, "This should be a day of rejoicing! Forty-three souls in heaven today!"

Two of the forty-three souls, it was found

out later, were camp administrators who had been preparing a list of accusations against the director. The charges included reports that he had molested several of the campers, also now deceased.

The minister and his wife who founded the camp and owned it were retired. When the news about the director broke, the minister shot his wife then blew his own brains out.

Those were the facts, but the tragedy lived on in the stories passed down and told around fires at other camps ever since. Everyone said the camp was haunted. I'd never believed those stories, until now.

Vincent said we were coming into Scatter's world," I said to Trey. "Why would he pick a place like this?"

We continued up the hill to the fence. Then we followed it to our left, looking for an entry. Inside were several buildings with fake log siding. The largest, in the center of the compound, was a sort of lodge, three stories high. On one side was a smaller building with a cross over the door. On the other was a rectangular structure made of brick. In front was an empty swimming pool with showers off to one side and a long, one-story building shaped like the letter *E*.

Where was a gate? It seemed like we had practically circled the camp, and there was no way in. I consulted the paw, and it pointed back at me. Somehow we'd missed the entrance. So we went back the way we had come until suddenly the paw was pointing straight down and pulling my hand to the ground. I didn't resist. I knelt down and watched the paw in my hand trace a symbol in the sandy ground. And the soil began to give way.

Trey jumped forward and put a strong arm around me as we sank into the swirling sand like stones in a giant hourglass. For a minute, darkness closed around us. Then, suddenly, we were standing on a concrete floor in a windowless cell with one lightbulb on the wall.

There was a door at the end of the room. We both ran to it, but it was locked. The paw was motionless. "Whose friend are you?" I said to it. "You're supposed to help us find Jake. Instead we're trapped like—"

"Rats!" Trey said, and I turned to see hundreds of them scampering out of the shadows toward us. Trey grabbed me and held me up in the air while the rodents attacked his legs, squealing and biting. He was doing his best to kick them away, but they were gaining ground. I was wondering how long he could protect his feet when I heard the sound of rushing water.

The rats squealed louder as torrents of cold water began filling the room. It rushed in from pipes somewhere in the shadows. I broke loose from Trey. In a few minutes the water was at chest level. Then the light shorted out. The rats were frantic, climbing on top of one another to escape drowning. One big one jumped on my head, and I slapped it off. Trey fought another one away from his face.

With six inches of airspace left, I had an idea. We had tried to force the door, forgetting what Vincent had said about Scatter's illusions. This time I grabbed the paw, took a deep breath, and dove underwater. I swam in the blackness toward what I hoped was the door. When I felt the handle, I touched it with the paw. I felt a little buzz of energy, grabbed the handle, and turned. It moved, but the door opened inward. The water in the room was pressing too hard against it for me make it budge.

Then I felt Trey behind me. He pulled on the door with all his might, and a crack opened. I could feel the water trying to rush out. I pulled off one of my shoes and jammed it in the space. Then Trey and I raced up for air.

The water slowly drained away. The rats vanished. Trey looked at me as if to say, "Are you okay?" I nodded.

Then we turned toward the door, where a man in a hood was standing. He gestured to us to follow and then went up a stone stairway. We came out in the middle of the campground.

The hooded man turned away and walked in the direction of the building with the cross. We started to follow, but he turned and shook his head before going in. I saw now that the cross had been altered from the one that had probably been there when Rock of Ages was operating. This cross was upside down.

A minute later we heard a voice that seemed to be coming through a loudspeaker. It sounded like an old man, tired and slow, his breathing heavy.

"Welcome, my children, to our evening gathering. As we begin, join your hands with each other and your minds with mine. For my thoughts are yours and yours are mine." He paused. "Tonight's reading is from the Book of Going Forth by Day."

Then another voice read: "The king rises into the heavens among the gods dwelling there. He sits on the great throne and decides the affairs of men. He gives you his arm and leads you into the sky."

I gripped Trey's arm so hard that he winced.

"What is it?" he whispered.

"The voice," I said through tears. "It's Jake."

I don't remember much about the next hour. The old man preached. From the way he called himself "God's chosen" and all, I guessed it was Scatter. The other memorable thing was how hard it seemed for him to speak at all. Otherwise, all I could think about was Jake. He was right here!

It was still dark when the sermon ended, although it must have been nearly morning. Trey and I ducked behind a shed just as the door of the church—or whatever it was— opened. Light streamed out, and several dozen of the hoods emerged. Jake may have been among them; I couldn't tell. They all headed for the E-shaped building on the other side of the swimming pool.

I felt the paw move. It was stretching toward the door the worshippers had just passed through. Trey and I walked to the door and entered a kind of foyer, like you'd see in a church. Then we went through one more door into just what you'd expect: rows of seats and an altar and pulpit in front. Above everything was a large, blank screen.

I'd never felt this frustrated. To be so close! The paw was still. It seemed to be right where it wanted to be. Suddenly the lights went off and the screen lit up. And there, looking at me, was my best friend. He was dressed in a long white robe and a round cap with a flat top.

"Dani," he said formally. "Welcome. Your friend?"

"Jake!" I yelled. "What the hell is going on here? Are you all right?!"

He smiled. A weird, ugly smile. "I'm . . . wonderful!" And then, "Why are you here?"

"Why am I here? I came to rescue you, to get you and your parents away from this Scatter guy! To get you back to Bridgewater! Vincent brought me your message . . ."

"My message. I believe I told you that I cared for you, and I was sorry we wouldn't see each other again. Of course there was much I didn't know then, but I don't recall asking you to come after me."

I was trying really hard to keep it together. I was afraid if I said anything more I'd start crying.

Jake blinked. "Your friend?"

"Trey Little," Trey said. "Dani didn't invite me, but I wanted to help her find you."

"Well, thank you," Jake said. "I'm sorry there wasn't any need. My father says you were both very brave. You passed many tests. He believes you were seeking to join our community."

"What does your father have to do with all this?"

"My father knows all. Scatter knows all."

"Jake, what are you talking about? Are you saying Scatter is your father?"

"Yes. That's why Philip betrayed him. Philip knew my mother had lain with Scatter. When he realized I was the result of that union, jealousy hardened his heart. He handed Scatter over to the police, then took my pregnant mother with him to the Middle East."

"When did you find out about this?"

"When I got here. Funny, I came looking for my parents and learned who my real parents were. That my real father is the Anointed One."

I felt completely empty. I was losing my best friend all over again to this insanity. Trey put a hand on my shoulder.

"You both must be exhausted," the Jake-thing said. "Someone will come in a moment and take you to your rooms. See that you get something to eat, clean clothes. Dani, I'll meet with you in the morning." The screen blinked off.

I lost it then. My shoulders started to shake, and I sobbed against Trey's chest. He held on to me until I could recover a little.

"Look, Dani," he said, "Jake—"

"That's not Jake!" I shouted at him.

"Exactly. This is a cult, Dani. Jake has bought into it. That doesn't mean you've lost him forever."

"But he says he's happy here!" I started to cry again.

"I know, I know. I have an aunt who joined a cult when she was sixteen. She disappeared for two years. When her parents finally found her, they actually had to kidnap her to get her home. And she kept trying to go back. It was almost a year before she turned back into the person they knew. Today she's a soccer mom."

The door to the lobby opened. Two people in hoods, apparently a man and a woman, stood waiting for us.

The hooded couple led us to the flat building where we'd seen the worshippers go earlier. Inside was a small room with some sort of reception desk. Doors on either side, labeled MEN and WOMEN, led to separate living quarters.

I squeezed Trey's hand and followed my attendant. The hall was just like you'd find in a college dorm. The woman showed me to a room. It was spare but clean, with a bed and a chair and a desk. She handed me towels and fresh clothes, then motioned for me to follow her. The bathroom and showers were at the end of the hall.

The place was cold, as if someone had the air conditioning going full blast, and the hottest I could get the water was still only warm. I wasn't about to complain, though. I scrubbed and soaked for a good twenty minutes before I finally began to feel clean. My heart was still aching, but I decided to set it aside until I saw Jake again. The clean clothing the woman had given me was, of course, a white robe with a hood. I wrapped my own stuff in a towel and took it to my room. On the desk was a turkey sandwich wrapped in cellophane, a bag of chips, a chocolate chip cookie, and a very cold can of soda.

I wanted to go to sleep instantly, to turn off the conversation with Jake like a light and put off all feeling till tomorrow. But I passed the night more like someone with a fever. Bad dreams alternated with painful moments of being awake. The worst dream started with the sound of crying.

There, standing in the corner of my room, was a girl of twelve or so. She was dressed in shorts and a T-shirt that said "Amazing Grace." She was rocking and sobbing, covering her face in her arms.

I got up and crouched down to where she was. "What's the matter, honey?" I asked.

She jumped at the sound of my voice, but when she saw me she threw her arms around my neck and started crying even harder. Her body was cold and wet. I held her, not knowing what to say.

Suddenly I felt a hand on my shoulder. It was a woman with white hair. She stared at me as if to say, "Can I help?" Then I noticed blood all over the front of her dress. A man was behind her, also old and also trying to comfort the girl. The top of his head was missing.

Then I was aware of the dead smell that had surrounded Trey and me the night before. The door of my room slowly opened, and I expected to see drowned children crowding in. Instead, a tall, black-haired man loomed in the doorway. His face was blurred, the way they blur a person's face on TV when they want to disguise him, and his voice was distorted.

The old couple cringed behind me as the tall man ordered the girl, "Come with me. Now."

The girl held me even tighter, but the man took her arm and began dragging her toward the door. I held on as tight as I could. Then there was a cracking sound, and the room was empty. The door was closed. In my hand I held the girl's severed arm.

Early in the morning a bell started ringing outside. I heard shuffling in the hall. I supposed Scatter's followers were going to their morning worship service. When the dorm was quiet again, I headed for the lobby. I saw a lone hooded figure standing outside. I hesitated for a moment until I realized it was Trey. I ran to him and we hugged hard.

"How was your night?" he asked.

"Not great." I wanted to tell him about my dream, but I didn't know where to start. "How about yours?"

"Cold," he said.

"I noticed that."

"And those imaginary rats? Check out these imaginary rat bites." He lifted the hem of his robe to show me a leg covered with red cuts and splotches.

"Trey!"

"It's okay."

"I didn't thank you for lifting me up down there," I said.

"Not a problem." He smiled. "Anything from Jake?"

"Not yet. I think everyone's gone to church, or whatever they call it."

We made small talk like that for an hour or so. Somewhere I could hear Scatter's voice droning through the loudspeaker. I was grateful that Trey kept me from thinking too much about what was coming up.

Then the hoods began returning. One of them, perhaps the woman who'd attended me the night before, walked up and gestured for me to follow her. Trey fell in next to me, but she pointed at him and shook her head.

"It's all right, Trey," I said. "Catch up with you later."

The woman led me to a high double door at the front of the lodge. As we got closer the door swung open. It closed behind us as we stepped into a small lobby with an elevator on one side. The other side opened into a big dining room. I tried to see the woman's face, but her hood was pulled forward and she seemed to avoid my glance. I did see her hands, though. They were gray and splotchy, like the freezer burn I'd noticed on Vincent, but worse. Her skin was actually decaying.

We walked across the dining room to a hallway and an office labeled "Camp Director." Inside, Jake sat behind a pine desk, wearing the robe and cap he'd had on the night before. When he saw me, he rose and came forward, his arms open. It felt like I'd been waiting for this forever. I ran to him, and we hugged a long time.

I heard the office door close. The woman had left. Jake led me to a sofa and we sat down.

Then—I couldn't remember this ever happening before—neither one of us seemed to know what to say. I'm sure my face was saying, "Explain yourself." His face looked sad. It seemed to say, "I doubt you'll understand."

Finally, I said what had been on my mind for weeks: "Why didn't you call me? I would have come with you."

"That's why I didn't call, Dani. Like I said, at the time I was afraid it would be dangerous. And it was all about my family. I didn't want to risk you getting hurt."

"You don't think it hurt me when you just disappeared?" I said.

"I'm sorry."

Another awkward silence.

"Tell me what happened, Jake."

"It was like I said. My parents—Philip and my mom—disappeared. Then Vincent showed up—I thought he was a friend then—and showed me how to travel to this world. I expected dangers, but I was welcomed like a hero and brought to this place to meet my father."

"So you believed all this? Just like that?"

"Oh, no. At first I thought the whole thing was crazy. I didn't know anything about Mom and Philip's days with Scatter. I was still on a rescue mission, just biding my time until I could find my . . . parents."

"What happened?"

"The more time I spent with Scatter, the more I began to realize who I am."

"And that is . . . ?"

Jake smiled and shook his head in a way I found annoying—and patronizing. "His child, of course. And as his child I am destined to rule at his right side and inherit his kingdom."

"Jake, your father's kingdom is a run-down summer camp and a few zombies in hoods."

"The faithful have endured many trials. They have trusted my father's promise. You see them now with earthly eyes. They look old. Their bodies are decaying."

"Jake, they're dead! They walk around, but they—"

"Oh no, they live. The freezing was hard on all of them, not the least upon my father himself, as you'll see. But this is temporary.

Scatter calls what happened in Bridgewater 'the first resurrection.' Soon there will be another, and we will all be glorified. But don't just take my word for it. I want you to meet my father."

Jake stood and took my hand. He led me to a closet where several robes hung. They were all white, of course, but made of heavy wool. "Put this on," he said, handing me one and putting on another himself.

We walked back across the dining room and got on the elevator. We went down a long way. As we dropped, the air got colder. By the time we stopped, I could see my breath. Finally the doors opened, and I was face to face with Scatter.

I felt sick to my stomach. This was the tall man in my dream.

Was this Jake's father? He was tall and thin, with Jake's features, but his head had been shaved. There were four bandages on his scalp. He was yellow around the eyes, and his skin was spotted with black and green and gray.

Scatter moved very slowly. He paused often to catch his breath, breath supplied by an oxygen tank on a cart next to him. When he opened his mouth, I could see that his teeth were yellow and sharp, like a wolf's.

It couldn't have been much above freezing in the room. Otherwise it was furnished like a luxury apartment without a view. Through a half-open door to one side I could see a large hospital bed, another oxygen cart, and some IV stands. In a corner in the living room were studio lights and a video camera on a tripod.

Jake bowed from the waist. Then he stepped forward and hugged his father, carefully. Scatter turned his eyes to me.

"Danielle," he said, trying to smile but clearly in pain. "Jake has spoken of you often. Come, sit."

We sat on a couple of loveseats arranged around a coffee table. Despite his physical weakness, Scatter's black eyes were fully alert. He looked me up and down, then focused all his attention on my face, as if he were trying to look into my soul.

"You and the young man who came with you . . ."

"Trey."

"Yes. You are very brave. You must care a great deal for my son. I can see why he has spoken so highly of you."

I didn't say anything.

"Very brave, and beautiful too," he went on.

Now he was creeping me out. I thought about the girl in my dream.

"You have joined our family at a momentous time. Have you told her, Jake?"

"Not completely, Father," Jake said. "I thought it best to leave that to you."

Then Scatter said the words I'd heard Jake read the night before: "The king rises into the heavens among the gods dwelling there. He sits on the great throne and decides the affairs of men. He gives you his arm and leads you into the sky."

Scatter looked at me intently. "I can see you doubt the word, Danielle. But don't judge by what you see. You are looking at a sick old man, I know. Do you know what happens when they try to preserve you cryonically? They drill holes in your skull and pump antifreeze into your veins. They freeze you slowly to minimize tissue damage. And they thaw you out the same way.

"The freezing preserved us for a time, but the thawing happened a little more, ah, quickly than would have been ideal. To put it simply, we're spoiling. The cold prolongs our existence here, but only briefly. Before long, in two days in fact, we will all ascend to the true kingdom. We will discard our tired bodies and shine like youthful gods!"

"How will that happen?" I asked.

Scatter's black eyes flashed. "In a flash of light! In a tower of fire! We will ascend the heavenly staircase to the true kingdom. We will be clothed in light and our souls will endure forever!"

All of a sudden, Scatter started to cough uncontrollably. Jake jumped up and found him a glass of water. When Scatter stopped coughing, Jake checked the oxygen tank and adjusted the nasal tubes. I heard footsteps in the bedroom, and a woman in a robe made of white fur came out.

"Hello, Dani." It was Jake's mom.

"Hello, Mrs. . . . ?"

"You can call me Bonnie." She kissed Scatter on the forehead, then came over and hugged Jake.

I could barely control myself. I turned to Scatter. "So you sent Vincent to get Jake? And then to get me?"

Scatter laughed. He started to wheeze, but recovered himself.

"Ah, Vincent," he said. "My poor, confused little brother! For a long time he was one of my most devoted followers. He was imprisoned at the same time I was, but he stayed loyal to me. When I was frozen in the government laboratory at Bridgewater, Vincent was happy to follow me even there, after his first death. But even in the early days Vincent was prone to these attacks of what he would call 'conscience.'

"After the first resurrection, we had a falling-out. He was opposed to anything he thought was motivated by revenge. 'Just build the kingdom,' he said. 'Forget about the past.' When he learned we were going to take Philip and Bonnie and Jake, he interfered. Because of his meddling, we didn't get Jake at first. And then he sent Jake here, believing his nephew could actually undo my plans."

"That's what I thought I wanted then, Dani," Jake interrupted. "The hard part was leaving you out. That's why I made the video. But Vincent was false. He pretended to help me, but he was actually hoping to use me against my father."

"When Jake didn't return," Scatter continued, "Vincent imagined some evil had befallen him. And being Vincent, he felt responsible. So he tried once more, Danielle, as you know."

"What happened to Philip?"

Jake and his mother looked at each other. Scatter's voice got harder. "Philip," he said, "is no longer among us."

By now I was suffocating in the weirdness. Jake had gone insane, just like his dying father—if, in fact, Scatter even *was* his father. Perhaps he had helped murder Philip. There was nothing I could do for Jake as long as we were in this place. Trey was right. We needed to get him home.

My heart fell into my stomach. Where was the paw?!

I tried as best I could to hide my panic. When "family time" was finally over and I was escorted away from Scatter's private quarters, I sprinted across the grounds to the dormitory and ran to my room. My old clothes were cleaned and folded on the bed, along with fresh towels. My jacket pockets were empty. The paw was gone.

For a while I just sat on the bed feeling sick. Every now and then I would go through the pockets again, as if the paw might magically appear there. Maybe it had fallen out. I looked under the bed, tore off the sheets. Nothing.

The laundry! There was a washing machine and dryer next to the bathroom. I ran down the hall to look. Both machines were empty. How could I have let our only chance of escape get away from me?

I wandered out of the dorm and walked in a trance around the grounds.

"Dani!" It was Trey calling. He walked up and put an arm around my shoulders. "How did it go?"

I shook my head.

"I'm sorry," Trey said, and I could tell that he really was. "While you were gone I snooped around a little and . . . . Hey, what's the matter?"

For the second time in twenty-four hours I was gasping and crying. I couldn't talk. I just sobbed and shook while Trey held me. Because of my carelessness, my stupid fixation on Jake, Trey was trapped here too.

I finally had to tell him. I explained a little about meeting Jake and Scatter, and about Scatter's latest prophecy. Then I told him about the paw and started to cry again. "I'm so sorry, Trey! It's my fault. Now we're stuck here. There's no way out!"

———

I think I expected him to be angry. Instead he put a hand on my cheek and made me look at him. With his other hand he wiped away the tears on my face. "There's always a way out, Dani. Maybe it's not as easy as we might have expected. But the way in here wasn't easy either, and we did it, together. We'll get out together too."

Then he leaned down and kissed me. I kissed him back. He took my hand, and now it was the two of us, walking aimlessly around the compound. We were probably doomed, but smiling and feeling, nevertheless, some kind of weird, out-of-place happy.

"Dani," Trey said finally, "do you remember at the club, when that guy Vincent showed up? You know what he said to me?"

"He said he told you something about yourself you thought nobody knew."

"He looked me straight in the eye and said, 'You hate yourself.' And he was right."

"Whatever, Trey . . . Are you serious?"

Trey smiled. "Yeah, I act just the opposite. Rich kid, football player, girlfriends, all that. But, I don't know, most of the time I just feel empty. Or I did. The last day or so, yeah, it's been a trip, but I've actually felt like I have a purpose, like I can help someone beside myself."

"I'm glad you're here," I said and squeezed his hand. And honestly, I really was.

After a while, Trey pointed at the brick building to the right of the lodge. "That's the power plant," he said. "There's a generator in there and barrels of oil to run it. It powers the air conditioning, the lights, the water pumps— everything. After the morning service, most of the hooded folks leave the compound. I'm not sure where they go. Judging by supper last night, there must be a convenience store around here somewhere."

I actually smiled.

Wherever the hoods went during the day, we learned that they could gather at headquarters quickly if needed. That afternoon an alarm like a storm siren sounded in the compound. Instantly, cult members came running from every direction and gathered in front of the building where the prayer services were held. Some of them had guns.

One with a large rifle seemed to be a kind of leader. He said something to the group and then whirled his right hand in a circle over his head. Apparently the gesture meant "Search the area," because that's what the members did. They spread out as if they knew their individual assignments. They had done this before.

"What's up, do you think?" I asked Trey.

He shrugged. "Maybe some kind of drill."

After half an hour they were back together again, shaking their heads. Then, at a signal from the leader, they went their separate ways.

"You know, Trey," I said, "when you think about it, except for the guys with guns, this place has pretty lousy security."

"Yeah," Trey agreed, "but who would want to break in here anyway?"

That night I prayed. I'm not a real religious person. Mom, Dad, and I go to Saint Matthew's, the Episcopalian church in Bridgewater, but only on Christmas and Easter. When I pray on my own, it's usually because I'm desperate or grateful. That night I was both.

"God, thank you for Trey!" I whispered. "I don't think I could face this without him. And please . . . . Please! Find a way for us—and Jake—to go home."

That night I dreamed of the drowned girl again.

Once again she was huddled, crying, in a corner of my room. I went over and sat down beside her, and she threw her arms around me as she had done the night before. I just held her. Suddenly I heard heavy footsteps in the hall. The girl started shaking and looking at the door. As we heard the lock turning, I jumped up and held myself against the door. Someone was trying to get in, someone very strong. I pushed back as hard as I could.

I tried to yell "Go away!" but I couldn't make a sound. Then in the distance I heard a voice. It was Jake. "Father?"

The pressure on the door stopped, and footsteps retreated down the hall. When I turned back, the girl was gone.

In the morning I found Trey out in front of the dorm. He kissed me as soon as I reached him. And then the loudspeaker began broadcasting Scatter's morning message:

"Children, we are on the brink of bliss. Prepare your souls! Let go of all your anxieties and look to me. One day from now—tomorrow!—we will all climb together into the sky. I will go to my palace, and I will take you with me!" And so on.

"What does that mean, Trey? Just that they'll all die and we'll be in this weird place alone?"

"I don't know. A lot of these guys make prophecies about the end of the world that don't turn out."

"I want us all to go home, Trey. You and me and Jake. Maybe once we're there, we can help him."

"That's what I want too, Dani. Don't worry. We'll figure out something."

That was when we noticed Jake advancing toward us. He hugged me and shook Trey's hand.

"How are the both of you?" he asked. "Is there anything you need?"

What the heck? "Jake, I need you to listen to me."

"Of course."

"Have you forgotten eight years of our being best friends?"

He sighed. "Dani, does being best friends mean we only do what the other one wants? Doesn't it mean we want the best for each other?"

"It means that when one of us is hurting, or doing something hurtful, the other one tries to help them."

"But I'm not hurting. I'm happy here."

"I don't think what you say you want is really your idea. It's something Scatter put there! Come back to Bridgewater with me. You're not yourself!"

"In fact," Jake said coldly, "myself is just what I am. What I was, what you know—I'm more than that now. I wish you could see that."

Jake turned to go, but then he stopped and turned back. "I want you both to have a chance to be with us forever. Join us! Think about it, please! I'll speak with you again in the morning." Then he bowed and walked off.

"He's so strange, Trey," I said.

"We need to get him away from all this," Trey agreed.

The problem, of course, was that we didn't even know how to get ourselves out of here.

"Maybe we could retrace our steps," Trey said. "Head up there," he pointed to the lake and woods outside the compound, "and then..."

"Even if we could," I said as sadness settled over me, "how could we drag Jake all that way if he didn't want to come?"

Then a voice right behind us made us jump.

"Maybe a tranquilizer? Something to put him to sleep?" There was no mistaking that whistle. It was Vincent!

"Don't act as if anything is unusual," he warned. "I'm just a member of the community standing near you." And that's what he looked like, another hooded figure, tall and thin, with scaly hands.

I faced Trey, as if we were just continuing our conversation, and said, "Vincent, how did you know . . . ?"

"Well," he said, "the cat's paw came back to me, so I knew you'd been separated."

"But you said you couldn't come into this world because—"

"Because my heart was heavy. And it was true. I was a slave to my anger toward my brother."

"He said you had a falling-out over kidnapping the Sawyers," I continued.

"I disagreed with that plan," he said. "I hoped the violence had stopped when the community broke up. But that wasn't the reason for my anger. Many years ago, our parents vanished without a trace. In due time, they were declared dead. Scatter inherited their property and used the money to start the community in New York.

"While I was in prison, I learned that my brother had had them killed. That destroyed me. I had always worshipped my brother. He was smarter than I was, with this incredible magnetism that drew followers to him. And he had a huge knowledge of magic and the spirit world, much of which he shared with me. He can move among worlds. He can control people's wills. He can summon storms—I can't do that one."

"Did he summon the storm in Bridgewater?" I was really thinking about the storm at Rock of Ages Bible Camp.

"Oh, yes. Before he was frozen, he chose the date and set the spell."

"And did he give you the paw?"

"Yes, and showed me how to use it. But the paw opens no gates for those with evil intentions. As long as I was dominated by anger at my brother, I could not follow him."

"He said you agreed to be frozen in Bridgewater in order to follow him."

"That was before I learned what he'd done. When I did learn, I shut him out of my life. It didn't seem that what would happen to my body mattered anymore. When I was resurrected, and Scatter was still in charge, I was stunned and afraid. And still angry."

"What changed?"

"I gained a higher purpose. At this point, Scatter will do what he will do. Which, I believe, is die. But I was responsible for sending three innocents here, and I realized it was my duty—

my higher purpose, if you will—to help them escape before doomsday. Once I gave up my anger and committed myself to that mission, the paw was happy to assist."

"Doomsday?" Trey and I asked at the same time.

"Children," Vincent began, "this world and everything in it—including you—is Scatter's dream. When the dreamer dies, everything in the dream ceases to exist."

"But Scatter says he's taking his followers into the sky with him tomorrow!"

"Scatter's prophecies are often imprecise," Vincent said, "but there's no reason for us to delay. I just need the three of you, you two and Jake, in one place."

"Jake will meet us in the morning," I said. "He wants us to join the cult."

"Perfect. Danielle, take this." He handed me a small leather bag. I peeked inside and saw a medical syringe filled with a clear liquid. "I'll watch," Vincent continued. "When you are together, you will need to administer the tranquilizer to Jake. Then I'll join you, and we'll all return to Bridgewater."

I didn't fully trust it, but still. . . . It was a plan.

Vincent wandered off. I felt hope in my heart again, and Trey was beaming.

"That's what happened with my aunt," he said. "They hired professionals who drugged her and then yanked her from the cult."

The rest of the day seemed to go too slowly. That night, I was afraid I'd be too jacked up to sleep. But I must have drifted off.

I felt something cold on my arm. As my eyes adjusted to the darkness, I saw that it was the hand of the young girl I'd watched Scatter abduct the night before. She motioned for me to follow her. We walked out of the dormitory, across the grounds, and out to the church. When we got there, she pointed to the front of her shirt, where it said "Amazing Grace." She pointed to the second word and looked at me.

"Your name is Grace?" I asked, and she nodded.

Then she pointed at the upside-down cross over the church door and frowned. She stood on tiptoes to reach it, but she wasn't tall enough. When she looked back at me, I knew what she wanted. I bent over so she could climb up on my back. Standing on my shoulders, she pulled the cross off the wall. Then she jumped down beside me. Over the door where the cross had been was the dark imprint of the upright cross where it had hung for decades before Scatter had reversed it.

Grace started across the camp again, and I followed her to the fence behind the lodge. Close to the ground there was a hole in the wire. The girl scrambled through and motioned to me to do the same. In a few minutes we were at the beach.

Suddenly the water began to foam. One by one, children came out from it and began swimming toward us. The smell of decay was overpowering. As the dead kids walked stiffly onto the beach, they lined up in front of Grace. Then the first child, a boy of ten or so, stepped forward.

Grace handed him the cross, and as she did she was transformed. The color returned to her skin, and her wet green hair turned blond. She was coming to life before my eyes! She turned to me with a huge smile. Then she pointed at the other children. As each one handed the cross to the next one in line, he or she would come to life like Grace. In just a few moments, I was surrounded by happy, living children.

When the last one, a very little girl, had been restored, she handed the cross back to Grace. Then every last child disappeared into the woods.

A soft, insistent knocking woke me from my dream. There was someone at my door.

"Who is it?" I said, I hoped not too loudly.

"It's me, Dani. Jake."

I went to the door and opened it. Jake gathered me in a hug. "Can I come in?"

"Of course." We sat down on the edge of the bed.

"Dani, you look at me as if I were someone you never knew."

I hesitated. "Honestly, Jake, since we came here, you seem like someone I never knew."

"If you love me . . ."

"I do love you, Jake. Why do you think I came here?"

"Then you should be happy for me. I've discovered the reason I was born!"

"To lead a cult?"

"To lead a people! To make their lives unimaginably better."

Hearing the friend I'd loved as a brother go on like this made me sadder than I'd ever felt before.

"Dani, have you thought about what I said this morning? Will you join us? Thinking that you won't be there with me—I've missed you so much!"

"I've missed you too, Jake." *And still do*, I thought. Then—this still hurts—for the first time in my life, I lied to him. "I'm still thinking about it," I said. "Find me in the morning."

"That's fantastic!" he said. His face lit up with hope, and my heart sank.

When he had left, I lay down and distracted myself by rehearsing the details of tomorrow's plan. I'd meet up with Trey. I'd have the needle ready. When Jake came to us, I'd look for Vincent. When I saw him approaching, I'd jab Jake.

What I didn't realize was that there was another person in the compound with his own plan. And that would change everything.

The morning began just as we'd expected. I
met Trey in front of the dormitory. During
the prayer service there were no hoods around,
but as they came out from the building where
they worshipped, I thought I spotted Vincent. I
felt in the folds of my robe for the syringe.

That's when I noticed that the cross over the
church door was gone.

Half an hour after the meeting, the main
door of the lodge opened, and Jake was walking
toward us. He was smiling broadly, spreading
his arms in welcome.

Suddenly an explosion rocked the grounds. I felt the pressure and the heat before I heard it. When I looked in the direction of the noise, I saw the brick building, the one with the power plant, in flames. Black smoke was already rising in a billowing column.

Jake's face showed panic. "What the—? The refrigeration! Father!" He turned to run toward the lodge just as a second explosion blew out its front door and flames began to consume the rest of the structure. Then we saw a man in a hood running toward the church. He threw something, and the third building exploded into smoke and flames like the other two.

At that moment a taller figure—I was sure it was Vincent—grabbed the man from behind and tried to restrain him. The shorter man was more powerful, though. He bulled Vincent to the ground. In the struggle, his hood fell off. It was Philip Sawyer.

"Jake," I yelled over the roar of the flames, "I thought Scatter said he was . . ."

"'No longer among us.' He escaped the compound. We'd been looking for him."

By now the cult members were mobilized. Jake, Trey, and I ran toward Philip and Vincent, but there was a solid wall of flame between us and the struggling pair. Meanwhile new explosions, probably the oil barrels in the first building, kept rocking the compound, spewing fiery debris in all directions. Some of it landed on the lodge, which burned now in several places.

When the hoods reached the flames, they milled around in confusion. That's when Philip produced a gun and started firing. Jake pulled me to the ground and covered me, but I could still see the struggle. Vincent grabbed Philip's left arm, but Philip spun around. There was a shot, and Vincent dropped to the ground.

"My father will die," Jake was saying, "just as he prophesied. We will enter the next kingdom in a flash of light and a tower of fire!"

I thought of Vincent's words: "This world

is Scatter's dream. When the dreamer dies, everything in it vanishes."

Abruptly, the shooting stopped. But the flames climbed. The heat was scorching, and the buildings were roaring as if they would collapse at any moment. Where was Trey?

"I'm okay, Jake," I shouted over the roar. "Let me up!"

When I stood up, I saw why the shooting had stopped. Trey must have dived straight through the flames. Now he was wrestling Philip, trying to get the gun away.

But Philip didn't plan to go up in smoke. He suddenly threw the gun away, and when Trey moved to get it, Philip ran instead to Vincent's body on the ground nearby. I think Trey realized it at the same moment I did: Philip was after the paw.

Ignoring the gun, Trey jumped on Philip again. By now, Scatter's dream was coming apart. The sky was dark with smoke, and the power plant rumbled louder than a train as it began to collapse. In places the flames rose hundreds of feet. Cult members on fire ran screaming in all directions. Jake and I watched Trey and Philip struggling and waited for the end.

Then, for a second, Trey got free of Philip's grasp. Philip still had the paw, though. He held it up and looked around for an exit. But Trey tackled him before he could find one. The jolt jarred the paw loose, and Trey quickly grabbed it.

The lodge was shaking and rumbling now. "Get out of here while you can, Trey!" I begged, but he couldn't hear me.

He could see me and Jake, though, shouting and waving at him through the flames. "Go!" I shouted.

But before Philip could attack him again, he reared back and threw the paw toward us with all his might. It landed at our feet. The lodge shuddered and started to implode. There was no time to think. I pulled out the tranquilizer and stabbed Jake's arm. His eyes widened, then he slumped to the ground. I held the paw, saw the air behind us turn to water, took one last look at Trey still fighting Philip, and dragged Jake through the gateway.

Next thing I knew I was standing in Folly

Park in Bridgewater. Jake lay unconscious at my feet. I had to go back and get Trey, even if it meant my life. But the paw wouldn't move. I held it up and waved it like a wand, but it might as well have been some stick I'd picked up.

Tears of frustration ran down my cheeks. Then grief. The dreamer had died. The world unlocked by the cat's paw no longer existed.

J ake came to after a few hours. By then I'd
sneaked into the locker room at the country
club, ditched the robe, and dressed in my own
stuff.

I wasn't sure how I would handle the "new"
Jake or how he would react to losing what had
become his dream. But Vincent had known
what he was doing. Whatever I had injected
into Jake was way more complex than just a
"tranquilizer." My friend had no memory of
Scatter's world or anything that had happened
there. He remembered missing his parents after
the storm. He also had a hazy memory of "an

older guy who wanted to help me find them,"
but that was all.

Of course the police were suspicious. They had
gotten calls from neighbors, the college, and
the supermarket. They knew how long Jake
and his parents had been missing. When Jake
suddenly resurfaced, he was a prime suspect
in his parents' disappearance. The police
questioned him repeatedly, and they thought
his "I don't remember" line was lame.

When Jake passed a lie detector test, they
sent him to a forensic psychiatrist. The shrink
said that the trauma of losing his parents had
probably caused "compensatory amnesia." That
meant Jake couldn't deal with the trauma at
first, so his memory shut down. This could have
happened even if Jake had killed his parents,
which is what the police suspected.

My first days back in Bridgewater, I could have
used a little compensatory amnesia myself. I

walked through my life like a dead person. I had no appetite. I couldn't sleep. And there was no one I could tell about what I was feeling. Not even Jake.

When my parents got home from their vacation, Mom saw my raccoon eyes and realized right away that something wasn't right with me. "Is there anything you want to talk to me about, honey?" she asked.

"No," I lied. "I'm okay. Just really wanting school to start."

That would happen in a week, and I still had that paper to finish. And a few more days of work at the club to put in. The warmth had returned, and the pool was crazy busy. It was all I could do to keep track of all the little kids tearing around and warn the middle-schoolers over and over again not to jump off the high dive till the water cleared below.

It was my fourth day home, and I was getting ready to open the pool. Kids and their parents were already lined up at the gate. When I finally unlocked it, they just about trampled me in their rush to the water. I had turned to head for my perch when I heard a voice behind me.

"Hey, beautiful."

"Trey? Trey?!" It was him! We wrapped our arms around each other. I was laughing and crying and dancing around. People watching probably thought . . . I didn't care what they thought.

"It's all right, Dani," Trey said finally. "It's all right."

"How?!" was all I could say.

Trey smiled. "Vincent. When I threw the paw to you, Philip went crazy. I think he wanted to strangle me. But Vincent had crawled to the gun, and when Philip lunged at me, Vincent shot him. I went to see what I could do for Vincent, but we both knew he was dying. Just as the lodge came down he said, 'Well done, Trey.' Then he put his hand on my forehead and said some words I didn't understand. The last thing he said was 'Safe journey.'

"I dunno. It seemed like I was back in Bridgewater right away. Apparently my 'safe journey' took a few days, though."

By the time school started, the police had backed off Jake a little. They had searched his house, his cell phone records, and the family car. They brought cadaver dogs to go over the entire property. They interviewed all his friends. Fortunately, I didn't have to face the lie detector. After all this, there was no evidence of foul play, so there was nothing to be done except keep Jake under observation. And Jake had a life to live in the meantime. So Mom and Dad arranged with the county social services to be his foster parents until he was eighteen.

Now he lives at our house, and it's just like

having a real brother. We're not sixth-graders anymore, though. I have something I never had before with Jake: a secret, a big one that I can never tell him about. He also will never know that I can't look at him anymore without seeing Scatter and knowing that half of my best friend's DNA comes from someone who was criminally insane.

Trey's parents were upset with him in the way parents are when you've frightened them. Everyone knew he had a lot of freedom, but he'd been out of touch for a week. His mom and dad had called the police and the hospitals, offered a reward for information—the whole thing. He gave them a pretty weak story about a wild party, friends from another state who needed a ride, another party, and a lost cell phone.

"I don't think they believed me, Dani," he told me. "But they're so grateful I'm safe, it's almost like they don't want to know the details. I wonder what they think really happened."

After a while they stopped asking questions, but they took his car away for the rest of the summer.

Trey and I are closer than ever now. But we never talk about our time in Scatter's world. A few days after we were reunited, we went out to Indian Pond, a small lake in the woods outside town. Trey threw the paw as far as he could into the water. I threw my white robe into a Dumpster at school. I hope no one shows up wearing it someday. And the DVD Jake made just before he disappeared? I broke it in a dozen pieces and put it in the trash.

Life is good. Most of the time I'm happy. I have a lot to be grateful for. But my heart, to use Vincent's phrase, is a little heavier now. Things aren't as simple as they used to seem. Maybe it's not even because of Scatter. Maybe it's just growing up.

Just before Thanksgiving, Bridgewater had a record warm spell. That week the mystery of the cryonics lab was "solved," according to police. Twenty miles into the woods outside town, some hikers stumbled on a scene out of a horror movie: twenty-nine decaying corpses near the site of the old Rock of Ages Bible Camp. The government had DNA from all the inmates frozen at the Institute for Cryonic Experimentation, and everyone was accounted for.

DNA technology being what it is, and with the location of the corpses reminding everyone of the Bible camp tragedy, forensic specialists began revisiting evidence from the site and from the child victims of the seventies. The police had kept clothing belonging to one of the girls who reported being abused by the camp director. When they reexamined it, they found DNA belonging to Scatter. After thirty-some years, they knew the identity of the camp director.

They also figured out which of the corpses, many of them by now just puddles of lumpy fluid, was his. There was a wooden cross planted in its chest.

I understand something now that I didn't before all this happened. We live in the present and we plan for the future. But the past—even if it isn't our past—can reach out like a cat's paw and change our lives.

Everything's fine in Bridgewater. Really . . .

Or is it?

Look for these other titles from the
Night Fall collection.

MESSAGES FROM BEYOND

Some guy named Ethan Davis has been texting Cassie.
He seems to know all about her—but she can't place him.
He's not in Bridgewater High's yearbook either. Cassie
thinks one of her friends is punking her. But she can't
ignore the strange coincidences—like how Ethan looks
just like the guy in her nightmares.

Cassie's search for Ethan leads her to a shocking
discovery—and a struggle for her life. Will Cassie be able
to break free from her mysterious stalker?

SKIN

It looks like a pizza exploded on Nick Barry's face. But
bad skin is the least of his problems. His bones feel like
living ice. A strange rash—like scratches—seems to be
some sort of ancient code. And then there's the anger . . .

Something evil is living under Nick's skin. Where did it
come from? What does it want? With the help of a dead
kid's diary, a nun, and a local professor, Nick slowly finds
out what's wrong with him. But there's still one question
that Nick must face alone: How do you destroy an evil
that's inside you?

THE CLUB

The club started innocently enough. Bored after school,
Josh and his friends decided to try out an old game
Sabina had found in her basement. Called "Black Magic,"
it promised the players good fortune at the expense of
those who have wronged them. Yeah, right.

But when the club members' luck starts skyrocketing—
and horror befalls their enemies—the game stops being
a joke. How can they end the power they've unleashed?
Answers lie in an old diary—but ending the game may be
deadlier than any curse.

THE PROTECTORS

Luke's life has never been "normal." How could it be, with his mother holding séances and his half-crazy stepfather working as Bridgewater's mortician? But living in a funeral home never bothered Luke. That is, until the night of his mom's accident.

Sounds of screaming now shatter Luke's dreams. And his stepfather is acting even stranger. When bodies in the funeral home start delivering messages to Luke, he is certain that he's going nuts. As he tries to solve his mother's death, Luke discovers a secret more horrifying than any nightmare.

UNTHINKABLE

Omar Phillips is Bridgewater High's favorite local teen author. His Facebook fans can't wait for his next horror story. But lately Omar's imagination has turned against him. Horrifying visions of death and destruction come over him with wide-screen intensity. The only way to stop the visions is to write them down. Until they start coming true . . .

Enter Sophie Minax, the mysterious Goth girl who's been following Omar at school. "I'm one of you," Sophie says. She tells Omar how to end the visions—but the only thing worse than Sophie's cure may be what happens if he ignores it.